D1129693

Mikey Makes The Team

Written by Susan Amundson • Illustrated by Brenda Geiken

ISBN 1-59984-015-4

Published by bluedoor, LLC
              6595 Edenvale Boulevard, Suite 155
              Eden Prairie, MN 55346
              800-979-1624
              www.bluedoorpublishing.com

Printed in the United States of America.
10 9 8 7 6 5 4 3 2 1

Dedication

For Sophia and children of all ages.

Today's the big day.
It comes once a year.
It's Game Day in Mrs. Bubble's
classroom at All Kids School.
This year, they'll play baseball.
Winners will get their names on a trophy.
Joey wants to win that Golden Trophy.
It will be displayed at school.
But he doesn't want Mikey on his team.
Mikey's leg doesn't work. He wears a brace.
He can't run.
He can only walk.

Joey, Linda, and Susie meet Khobi and Hero walking to school. Joey trips and falls flat on his face. He doesn't see the bump in his way. He's thinking about that trophy. He's sure he can win it this year. But Mikey can't be on his team. He can't run the bases like the other kids.

"I see my name on the trophy,"
Joey says picking himself up off the ground.
"Mine, too!" Susie shouts. "And me," Linda yells.
"But Mikey can't be on our team!"

Khobi states, "I don't care if my name is on
the trophy. Neither does Hero.
And Mikey can be on my team...
even if his leg doesn't work.
In my land, everyone
gets to play in a game.
That helps build
friendships."

They arrive at school, excited for this big day. Loud voices are heard in their classroom. They see why. Mikey's name is on the blackboard...along with Joey's, Linda's, Susie's, and Khobi's.

"Mrs. Bubble put Mikey on our team!" Susie groans.

Everyone hushes...

"Tee hee," a classmate laughs. "You get Mikey."

"Not Mikey," Joey whispers.

Maybe Mikey's leg doesn't work, but his ears do. He can hear, "Not Mikey! Not Mikey!" He's heard that so many times.

"Boys and girls...let's go outside," directs
Mrs. Bubble. "The snow has been shoveled.
The ball field is cleared.
So find your team."

Mikey's teammates pout, as they walk out
to the ball field. They can't win with
Mikey on their team. They'll lose for sure.
Their names won't be on the trophy.
Not this year. Not ever.

But Khobi doesn't feel
that way. He speaks loud
enough for everyone to
hear. "Mikey, I'm glad
you're on my team."
Hero runs beside the kids.
He's happy, too!

The game begins. Everyone has fun playing ball, even Mikey's teammates. Suddenly, the scoreboard shows the game is tied.

A player from the other team points to Mikey. "Wait! He needs a turn." He knows if Mikey takes a turn, Mikey's team won't win. Mikey's team knows that, too. Mikey can't run. He can only walk. Mikey feels bad. He doesn't want to make his team lose.

Khobi has an idea. "I haven't had a turn, either. I'll share mine with Mikey."

"Huh? What do you mean?" the kids ask Khobi. No one has ever offered to share a turn.

Khobi explains, "Mikey can hit the ball.
He has strong arms. I'll run the bases.
I have strong legs. I will have a half turn.
Mikey will have a half turn.
Two half turns make one whole turn."

The teams talk.
They decide to try
Khobi's idea...

Mikey steps up to the plate.

"Strike one!" the ump hollers.

The other team laughs.

"Strike two!" Mikey waits too long.

His teammates are nervous.

"That's okay, Mikey," says Khobi.

"You can do it. Just smack that ball!"

The pitcher throws the ball for the third time. Mikey swings the bat. It connects with the ball. The ball flies high, higher, highest. It goes farther than any other ball hit. Then down, down it goes, almost over the fence, almost a home run. A player jumps to catch it. He misses the ball.

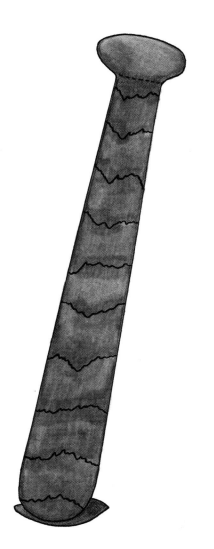

"Yeah!" Mikey's team cheers. "Run, Khobi! Run!"

Khobi's strong legs touch first base. Then he touches second base, third base, and on to home plate.

By now a player has the ball in his glove. He chases Khobi close to home plate.

Then something happens...

Hero adds himself to the game. He doesn't want Khobi chased. He runs after the player with the ball. He catches him. He jumps on him, knocking him to the ground. Then Hero licks the player's face. Slurp, Slurp!

A big cloud of dust hangs over home plate.
No one can see anything for a short time.
Then everyone can see again.
Khobi is on his tummy touching home plate.

The ump almost calls, "SAFE!"
But he sees there's no ball.

Everyone looks for the ball.

Hero barks, "Whrff! Whrff!"
He gets their attention.

The kids see Hero sitting by Mikey.
Hero has the ball. It's his.
No one can have it. No one.
Seeing Hero claim the ball makes the kids laugh.

Mrs. Bubble looks at her watch.
"It's time to go inside, kids.
The next class will be coming to use the field."

"Guess the game's over," says Joey.
"But who won?"

Again, the teams talk...

Mikey hit the ball farther than anyone
ever has. "He's the BEST!"

"I'm the BEST?"
Mikey thinks to himself.
He's never heard that before.

Khobi ran VERY, VERY, FAST.

Mikey's half turn and Khobi's half turn
made the strongest, fastest whole turn.

But which team gets the trophy with their names on it? There's no ball on the plate. That means no win and no out.
The ball is claimed by Hero.
He's not giving it up! It's his.

The children think...

Then, Khobi speaks out.
"When everyone is kind, everyone wins."

Khobi teaches the children something new about winning. Something they will remember. Khobi was kind and shared his turn.

This year the Golden Trophy has no names. Instead, it reads:

TEAMWORK
BUILDS
WINNERS

When the children see the trophy on display, they are reminded:

EVERYONE SHOULD HAVE A CHANCE TO PLAY IN THE GAME!

The Khobi and Hero Song

Words and Music by Susan Amundson
Transcription by Becky Raimann

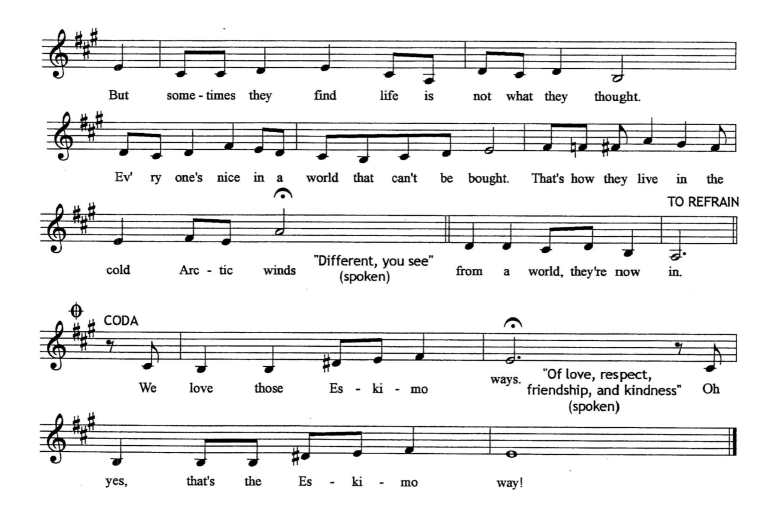

About the Author

Susan Amundson, author, first-time grandmother, and mother of three adult children, remembers writing stories as early as age seven. She worked with elementary-aged children for twenty-one years as an EMT. Doing intense research on the Samoyede Tribe and living with Samoyed dogs for 40 years gave Susan the insight to write The Khobi Hero Series. Each book of the series has a message that resonates with children of all ages. Susan lives in Minnesota with her husband of thirty-five years.

About the Illustrator

Brenda Joy Geiken has enjoyed a passion for art since childhood. She graduated in 1992 with an art degree from Northwestern College in St. Paul, MN. Brenda currently resides in Minnesota with her husband and daughter.

Brenda says, "The Khobi Hero Series has been a joy for me to illustrate."

The art for Mikey Makes the Team is rendered in watercolor and ink.

Endorsements

"Through her characters Susan Amundson speaks to the journey every child must make...."

Michael Donndelinger, MD, Child & Adolescent Psychiatrist

"Susan's books should be in every elementary school library."

Dr. Corolyn Mortensen, Ed. D.